Robbie Paterson

ABOUT THE AUTHOR

Phyllis Arkle was born and educated in Chester but since 1959 has lived in the Thames Valley village of Twyford.

She is a member of the W.I. and enjoys writing and reading. Her other interests include music and bridge.

Walking, especially in the Lake District, is a favourite pastime.

The Railway Cat
on the Run

Phyllis Arkle

Illustrated by Stephanie Hawken

Hodder
Children's
Books

a division of Hodder Headline plc

Contents

1

The Regatta

'Now then, Alfie, out of my way!' cried Hack, the Leading Railman. The handsome grey and white striped station cat took no notice.

'Don't forget, *I'm* in charge when Fred's away,' Hack went on. 'Go and catch some mice. That's your job.'

Alfie looked down his nose and twitched his tail. Hunger made him determined to stalk Hack until the stupid man served his supper. Thank goodness Fred would be back tomorrow, he thought. Fred, the Chargeman, was Alfie's greatest friend. He never kept Alfie waiting.

'I'll see to you later, nuisance,' shouted Hack, red in the face, as he strode off down the platform. Alfie followed, but it was not until after the last train had departed that Hack condescended to place a saucer of catmeat and a saucer of milk in front of the railway cat.

'I've half a mind to close the ventilator so that you can't squeeze out and sneak off somewhere,' grunted Hack as he went out and locked the staff-room door behind him.

'Miaow!' Good riddance, Alfie called after him. He soon finished the meal. Not a patch on Fred's food, he decided.

Then, determined to look his best for Fred tomorrow, he licked himself all over before settling down in his basket.

He thought about Hack. Not a bad fellow really, but short-tempered and, worst of all, could never see a joke. Alfie didn't know why he was always in Hack's bad books.

It occurred to Alfie that Hack had been acting in a very strange manner during Fred's absence. Once or twice he had caught the man doing press-ups and knee-bending exercises when he thought no one was looking, and Alfie had seen him sprinting up and down the platforms.

The Leading Railman had been furious when he noticed Alfie watching him. 'Spying on me again, you good-for-nothing cat,' he had cried.

But never mind about Hack, thought Alfie, yawning widely. Instead he would think of Fred and good times ahead at the station.

First, Fred would be back on duty in the morning. Then on Wednesday afternoon there was the annual regatta at the small riverside town five miles away at the other end of the branch-line.

Alfie had never been to the regatta. But he knew there was racing on the river and fun and games in the meadows, as well as fireworks in the evening. It was Alfie's ambition to join in the festivities. Each year he had tried to board a train bound for the regatta, but Hack was always on hand to grab him and hold him until the train had departed.

But Alfie was determined that, by hook or by crook, he would go to the regatta this year. With this thought in mind he turned over once or twice before falling into a deep sleep.

He was up bright and early next morning. A squeeze through the ventilator and a scramble over a fence took him to the station forecourt. He sat down, tall and neat. Soon the milkman came along in his lorry. 'Hello, Alfie,' he cried cheerfully. 'Up before times, aren't you? Waiting for Fred?'

'Miaow!' said Alfie, as he weaved in and out of the man's legs.

The milkman laughed as he placed four cartons of milk at the station gate. 'Good job these are not glass bottles, eh, Alfie,' he joked. 'You'd soon knock one over, wouldn't you?'

'Miaow!' cried Alfie indignantly. I've grown out of those silly pranks.

The man picked up another carton, opened it and poured the contents into a plastic bowl, which he placed in front of Alfie. 'That will keep you going until Fred arrives,' he said. 'I'll collect the empties on my return journey.'

'Miaow! Miaow!' cried Alfie. Thank you. He bent down and started lapping. Just what I needed, he thought.

It was not long before he heard a familiar sound and Fred came into view on his new motor-bike. Alfie rushed out to greet his friend.

'Careful, Alfie!' shouted Fred as he slowed

down to walking pace. 'Surely you haven't forgotten about road safety?'

'Miaow! Miaow! Miaow!' cried Alfie. Not me. He could hardly contain his excitement.

Fred parked his machine. He bent down and gently pulled Alfie's ears and stroked him under the chin. Alfie purred and purred.

'Has Hack looked after you properly?' asked Fred.

'Miaow-ow-ow . . .' said Alfie. Well . . . yes . . . when he wasn't jumping about in a ridiculous manner. He's up to something. I'm sure of that. You'll soon see.

'Breakfast first, Alfie,' said Fred.

Soon the railway cat was enjoying a tasty meal of liver and lights and another saucer of milk. When he had finished he stretched out, clenching and unclenching his paws, before rolling over and over on his back with his paws in the air.

Fred laughed. 'Missed me, haven't you. Alfie? Never mind, we're on duty together now.'

Alfie noticed Brown, the Booking Clerk, coming down the road and soon Hack appeared. The first passengers arrived, a train drew up and the day's business began. Commuters, school children and shoppers, Alfie greeted them all.

He stayed close to Fred, following him about the station. At last Fred exclaimed, 'For goodness' sake, Alfie! I'm not leaving you again until my next holiday. Follow Hack for a change.'

He looked round. 'Where is the man?' he said. Hack was not in sight, but faint sounds of music could be heard.

'What's going on?' said Fred as Alfie led the way to the staffroom.

Fred pushed the door open and Hack was revealed doing physical jerks in time to the radio.

'What on earth do you think you are doing?' bellowed Fred as he switched the radio off.

'Well, er – er – er, I'm just keeping fit – it's all the rage now,' mumbled Hack.

'Well, keep fit somewhere else and not in railway time,' ordered Fred sternly.

Hack paid more attention to his duties for one day, but next morning Alfie noticed him jogging across the footbridge and back. 'Miaow!' said Alfie to Fred, who was standing beside him.

Fred glanced up and saw Hack. But this time he smiled. 'He has entered for an amateur canoe race at the regatta,' he said. 'I'm allowing him half a day off on Wednesday.'

'Miaow!' cried Alfie, amazed. Hack in a race – impossible! The man only had one speed – s–l–o–w!

'We'll leave him alone, so long as he doesn't neglect his duties, shall we, Alfie?' said Fred.

'Miaow!' sang Alfie. Certainly. What a lark – Hack in a race! He was more determined than ever to get to the regatta.

For the next few days Alfie was on his very best behaviour and once Hack actually smiled and nodded his approval.

Fred came up at that moment. 'Glad to see you two on good terms for a change,' he said.

'Oh, he's all right, I suppose,' said Hack, 'but

I must make absolutely sure he doesn't get to the regatta. He'd only cause trouble. He must be locked up.'

'That would be useless,' laughed Fred. 'Alfie is as good as Houdini for escaping. I'll keep watch until the train departs. He won't get past me, I can assure you.'

'I wouldn't bet on it,' said Hack.

'Miaow!' hissed Alfie. I've got a plan.

On Wednesday morning Hack rushed about anxiously, getting on everyone's nerves.

'Oh, really, Hack, calm down,' said Fred. 'You'll be too tired to step into a canoe, never mind race in it.'

Hack mumbled something, then burst out, 'That cat has been sitting near the booking-office all morning. He's up to no good.'

'Alfie isn't likely to need a ticket to get to the regatta,' said Fred, grinning.

By this time Alfie was feeling nervous. Would his plan work?

Then about five minutes before the regatta train was due Alfie heard a familiar voice coming from the direction of the booking-office.

'The usual, please, Mr Brown,' said Mrs Pomeroy, briskly.

The Regatta

Alfie sighed with relief. He knew that the old lady always went to market on the twelve o'clock train on Wednesdays. The regatta would not put her off.

Mrs Pomeroy was Alfie's favourite passenger (not only because she always brought him a titbit from the market!). She was old, but in Alfie's opinion, smart. She dressed in long, full skirts and always wore a large hat. As usual she carried a wicker basket, which sometimes contained items she had collected for a charity shop in the town.

Alfie followed her on to the platform. She put

down the basket, with the old clothes inside. Alfie's luck was in!

Fred came up and greeted Mrs Pomeroy. Alfie took the opportunity (when they were not looking!) to scramble into the basket and hide under a woollen pullover.

Hack emerged from the staffroom dressed in blue blazer and white shorts. He glanced round. 'Where's that cat? He was here a few minutes ago. He'll be up to his usual tricks trying to board the train. I'll teach him, I'll . . .'

'Well, Mr Hack,' said Mrs Pomeroy reprovingly, 'Alfie was certainly here a few minutes ago, but if you have been tormenting him again it's small wonder that he wants to avoid you.'

'Tormenting him? Me? *He*'s the tormentor, not me!' yelled Hack.

'Control yourself, Hack,' said Fred sharply.

The train was approaching. 'Carry Mrs Pomeroy's basket,' he ordered.

Still looking round for Alfie, Hack picked up the basket and moved towards the train.

Hack was puzzled. 'You shouldn't carry such a weight, Mrs Pomeroy,' he said.

Alfie moved slightly. Hack stopped. He put the basket down, threw the pullover aside, grabbed

Alfie and thrust him into Fred's outstretched arms. He jumped into the train after Mrs Pomeroy, carrying the basket. He stood by a window and shook a fist at Alfie as the train moved off.

And Alfie sadly faced the fact that he would not be going to the regatta this year.

2

Wagon and Horses

'Really, Alfie, I'm surprised at you,' said Fred as the railway cat struggled out of his arms. 'I've told you time and time again that you are not going to the regatta.'

With tail held high Alfie stalked away and leaped lightly on to a seat on the main platform. He turned round three times before settling down with his face to the wall. He hadn't been there long before someone came up and stroked him from head to tail. Alfie made no response.

A young voice spoke. 'What's the matter with Alfie, Fred?'

'Oh, take no notice,' replied Fred. 'He's sulking. He'll get over it by suppertime.'

'Brrr . . . brrr . . . brrr . . . !' growled Alfie. Sulking, indeed! Get over it by suppertime! How insulting. He'd show them. He'd run away – leave the station for good. Fred could get another cat. Mind you, he'd never find such a conscientious cat as Alfie – so helpful, so popular with passengers and staff (except one member!).

So . . .

Alfie raised his head and pricked up his ears when he heard a familiar sound – clip-clop-clip-clop. He bounded off the seat and rushed out of the station just as a bright-red painted wagon, pulled by two fine heavy horses, drew up in front of him.

Alfie's old friend, Farmer Victor, jumped down. 'Hello there, Alfie,' he called. 'Come to meet Ben and Jake?'

'Miaow! Miaow!' Yes, sang Alfie as he looked up at the horses.

Alfie guessed that the farmer had come to meet a group of people – no more than twenty – off a train from London. During the summer months the farmer was a regular visitor to the station. To raise money for a children's charity, he organised trips in his wagon through lovely countryside with its villages and ancient inns, and including a good meal at the farm.

Alfie made up his mind. Here was a golden opportunity to escape. He would stow away on the wagon until it reached the farm. There he would stay. He would be the best farm cat in the county, perhaps the best farm cat in the country.

When the farmer went to welcome his passengers Alfie jumped up on to the wagon and scrambled into a corner underneath a wooden bench. How he wished he could travel on top of the seat, sit up high as the passengers did and marvel at the scenery and wildlife.

The passengers climbed on to the wagon, exclaiming how much more exciting it was travelling in a wagon instead of being driven in a car. The farmer joined them, took up the reins and they were off.

Everyone sounded jolly, but Alfie was very uncomfortable. He settled down to make the best of the journey. To his surprise the wagon did not rattle or shake very much. Apparently the country lanes had good surfaces. It felt as smooth as travelling on a main road.

He soon fell fast asleep, waking up when the wagon jolted over rough ground and came to a halt – probably stopping at an inn for some light refreshment. He raised his head. It must be a very popular inn, he decided, as he listened to sounds of merriment, music and shouting.

Alfie waited as one by one the passengers left the wagon. He heard Farmer Victor announce, 'Don't forget to take your sandwiches with you. Meet here in three hours time and we'll be on our way to the farm – for a super meal.'

When he thought the coast was clear, Alfie poked his head out, but the farmer saw him immediately. 'Well, well, well,' he exclaimed. 'If it isn't Alfie. I had no idea you wanted to come to the regatta.'

Alfie looked up, surprised. 'Miaow?' he said. The *regatta*? He jumped on to a bench and looked round. He saw marquees on the meadow and crowds of happy, excited people lining the riverbank shouting encouragement at the racers. How wonderful. He'd go and look for Hack straight away. He made a movement to jump down, but the farmer grabbed him.

'Oh, no, you don't,' he cried. 'Fred would never forgive me if you were lost or injured. So you stay with me. No arguing. Understand? I've promised to cheer for Hack in his race. You'll have to come along with me, like it or not.'

'Miaow!' sang Alfie. Best news I've heard for a long time.

Still clutching Alfie, Farmer Victor managed to open a toolbox and take out a collar and lead. 'Always keep these handy, just in case they're needed,' he said.

Alfie made no protest when the collar and lead were fastened round his neck (although he hoped that he would never again have to suffer such an indignity). The farmer left the horses in charge of a young man and then led Alfie towards the river.

'Hello, Alfie, what are you doing here?' called a man, laughing. 'Will the trains manage to run without you in charge at the station?'

It was nice to be recognised, thought Alfie, who was thoroughly enjoying himself. He glanced towards the river and saw tanned young men rowing as though their lives depended on it. But there was no sign of Hack.

Farmer Victor stopped to examine a programme of events. 'We're just in time,' he told Alfie. 'Hack's in the next race. We'll find a suitable position and cheer as he passes us. Come on.'

Willingly Alfie trotted along behind his friend as they made their way along the riverbank. The farmer stopped. 'This will do,' he said. 'Don't forget to give a good loud "MIAOW" as soon as he comes into view.'

Alfie doubted he would be heard among the noisy crowd, but he'd do his best. It seemed a long time before the canoe race was announced. But then there were shouts of, "Here they come!"

In his excitement Alfie strained at the lead and moved nearer to the river. But the farmer held on to the lead. 'Careful, Alfie,' he cautioned. 'Can't risk the railway cat drowning.'

The cheering was deafening as the racers came into view. Alfie soon saw that Hack, puffing and blowing, was lagging behind his fellow competitors. The railway cat could contain himself no longer. Breaking loose from his friend, he rushed down to the water's edge, miaowing and hissing for all he was worth.

People began to laugh loudly at his antics. Unfortunately Hack glanced towards the bank as

he passed. A scream was heard, then, 'It's that CAT!' Hack lost control and let go of his paddle.

Alfie stood rigid. What had he done? He'd only wanted to help. He couldn't bear to look. In a panic he ran off as fast as he could across the meadow. He could hear the farmer calling, 'Catch that cat!' But Alfie kept on running and disappeared into a nearby thicket. Never had he felt so miserable.

He crawled under a thick bush and sat down. One thing was certain, he could never go back to the station. Hack had undoubtedly lost the race and he, Alfie, would be blamed and never forgiven. Fred would be angry with him. No one would believe he had wanted to help Hack. He was sorry he'd ever heard of the regatta.

He couldn't think why he had wanted to run away from his duties as the railway cat. Fred was the best friend in the world. The railway cat lay still for a long time.

When the sun was setting he got up, stretched out and sharpened his claws on the rough ground before moving on. Progress was slow and he was beginning to feel tired and hungry. He started down a rutted track with grass growing down the middle and came across a gypsy encampment in a clearing.

He halted, undecided. Would the gypsies be kind? He took a chance and, despite the collar and lead round his neck, managed to get over the gate. Immediately, pandemonium broke out as two lurcher dogs, barking threateningly, leaped towards him.

But help was at hand. As Alfie quickly took refuge halfway up a tree two youths came running to his aid. The dogs were caught and tethered while one of the youths climbed the tree and carried a frightened Alfie down to safety. Several gypsies had emerged from their caravans to see what all the commotion was about.

'Here you are, Zendra,' said the young man holding Alfie. 'You've been wanting a cat so here he is – complete with lead.'

An old woman came forward and took hold of Alfie. 'He's a very handsome cat,' she said. 'I'll certainly keep him.'

She undid the collar and examined it. 'No identification,' she said. 'Collars are for dogs. His owner does not deserve to keep a pet.'

Oh dear, that's not true in my case, thought Alfie. But he liked the look of his new owner.

She reminded him of Mrs Pomeroy. He was content to be carried up a flight of wooden steps into her caravan.

Alfie looked round the neat, colourful interior. He noticed a crystal bowl on a small table and a long black and red cloak hanging on a hook.

'I hope you will enjoy being a gypsy fortune-teller's cat,' said Zendra, smiling.

'Miaow!' said Alfie. I'll do my very best.

If he couldn't be the railway cat he might as well be the gypsy cat. It would be a grand life, travelling round the country, jolly company, plenty of fresh air – but in his heart he knew he would always be the railway cat. If only he had not upset Hack, if only he had tried to get on better terms with the man, if only . . .

But it was useless crying over spilt milk. He would try and be the best gypsy cat in the country.

'Supper won't be long,' announced Zendra. Soon she put a dish in front of Alfie. 'Fresh from the river this morning,' she told him.

'Miaow!' said Alfie gratefully as he started on the fish. Very good, excellent in fact, he decided. A saucer of milk followed. 'Straight from the cow,' said Zendra.

When he had finished Alfie sat down and started to clean his face, his whiskers and ears before dealing with the rest of his body.

The gypsy watched, with a smile on her face. 'What a very clean cat you are now,' she said when he had finished.

'Miaow!' agreed Alfie. A good railway cat – he corrected himself – a good gypsy cat must always be well groomed.

3

A Gypsy Cat

First, Alfie had decided that he would stand no nonsense from the dogs. So, if one threatened him by coming too close, Alfie would arch his back until his hair stood on end, narrow his eyes and hiss. If that had no effect he would give the dog a quick right and left to the nose with a paw.

But it soon became a game. If play got out of hand Joe or one of the other gypsies would call out, 'That's enough, you rascals,' and play would cease for a time. Alfie would return to Zendra's caravan to sit quietly at her feet as she gazed into a crystal ball and told a client what to expect in the future.

'What a handsome cat he is,' remarked one visitor.

And another, 'He's certainly well trained.'

Zendra would smile and say, 'I'm very lucky to have such a clever, sensitive animal as a companion.'

Alfie would purr contentedly, happy to know that someone appreciated him. (Never mind what Hack thought.)

But, although there was never a dull moment in Alfie's new life, he was not entirely happy.

He pricked up his ears every time he heard a hoot or a whistle from a train travelling on the railway line about half a mile away. By the sound of wheels on the track he could distinguish between passenger trains (express or local) and goods trains. Then he couldn't help thinking with longing of Fred – and even of Hack! – and his duties as the railway cat.

Several weeks passed. One day, after a fortune-telling session, Joe came into the caravan. He opened up a newspaper and handed it to

Zendra. 'Read that,' he said, pointing to a particular item on the page.

Zendra read – and then was silent for a time. She looked up at Joe. 'It's him all right,' she said with a sigh. 'And he's just the most intelligent and companionable animal I've ever met.'

'But he's never really settled down here,' said Joe.

Could they possibly be talking about him, thought Alfie?

Zendra glanced at the paper again. 'I see there's a reward offered for any information as to his whereabouts.'

There was silence, then Joe said slowly, 'We'll have to let him go, I suppose.' He paused. 'Or shall we pretend we haven't read the–?'

'No, no,' said Zendra quickly. 'That wouldn't be fair.'

'All right,' said Joe reluctantly. 'We'll leave it until morning.'

Alfie spent a restless night.

Next evening when he had just finished supper and was busy cleaning himself, there was a knock on the door. Alfie stopped licking his left hind leg as he stared at the door.

Zendra looked down at him. 'I think someone

is coming to see you,' she said with a sigh. 'Come in,' she called.

And Fred entered. Alfie started to make a mad rush towards his friend, but checked himself by weaving in and out of Fred's legs while purring loudly.

Fred greeted Zendra, then bent down and stroked Alfie. 'Hello, old chap,' he said. 'What on earth have you been up to?'

He turned to Zendra. 'I've put a notice about him in the newspaper every week since he was missing.'

'But we rarely see a copy of this particular newspaper,' Zendra told him.

'Well, Alfie can count himself a very, very fortunate cat to have found you to look after him,' said Fred. 'I cannot thank you enough.'

'But it's been a pleasure,' said Zendra.

'Miaow!' put in Alfie. I've enjoyed myself too.

'I must pay you for looking after him, feeding him, and so on,' said Fred, getting out his wallet.

'No, no,' said Zendra. 'Certainly not. He has more than paid for his upkeep. I've never come across such an intelligent, obedient, clev—'

'Shush, please!' said Fred, smiling. 'He'll be getting conceited.'

'Not Alfie,' said Zendra firmly. She added, 'I like the name Alfie. It suits him.'

Alfie jumped up on to Zendra's lap and pushed his head under her chin. She stroked him. 'Now, I suppose I'll have to make inquiries about another suitable cat,' she sighed. 'But I'll never, never find one quite like the railway cat.' She gently pulled Alfie's ears. 'He's exceptional,' she added.

'Wait a minute,' said Fred as he made for the door. Alfie was ready to leap down but Fred put

out a hand, 'No, no,' he said. 'Don't get alarmed. I'll be back in a jiffy.'

Alfie settled down again and soon Joe came in, followed by Fred.

Joe was hiding something in his arms. 'Off you get,' he said, bending down and giving Alfie a gentle push with an elbow.

Alfie jumped down and Joe placed a sleek, all-black kitten on Zendra's lap.

She started in surprise. The kitten looked up at her, began to purr, then turned full circle and plopped down.

'Joe told me when he phoned last night about Alfie that you would need another cat,' said Fred. 'But it would have to be an intelligent and agreeable animal.'

'Miaow!' put in Alfie. Just like me, in fact!

Fred continued. 'I remembered that Farmer Victor was seeking a home for a kitten and here he is. His name is Blackie. I hope you will find him satisfactory, Madame.'

Zendra gently stroked Blackie from head to tail. 'Thank you,' she said. 'I'm sure we'll get on famously together.'

'Well, that's a relief,' said Fred. 'Are you ready to come home, Alfie?'

'Miaow!' said Alfie. Try and stop me!

'Well, say thank you to Zendra and wish her luck with Blackie,' said Fred.

Alfie nearly burst his lungs as he purred his thanks.

Soon, Fred and Alfie were on their way home. Alfie had enjoyed staying with the gypsies, but he was sure he had never felt happier in all his life than when he was sitting in the front passenger seat of Fred's car and listening to his friend's voice.

'We've missed you, Alfie,' said Fred. 'It's not like you to run away.'

'Miaow!' cried Alfie. I wasn't running away from *you*.

He wondered how Hack would greet him and whether he had persuaded everyone that he, Alfie, was a disobedient, disagreeable cat.

He lowered his head as they turned down Station Road.

'Nearly there,' said Fred. 'Wait till Hack sees you!'

'Miaow,' whispered Alfie. That's what is worrying me.

Meanwhile, there was great excitement at the station as news spread that Alfie might be on his way home by now. Everyone hoped the cat which Fred had gone to see would turn out to be Alfie.

Fred drew up in front of the station and a small group of people surged forward to welcome him.

Fred carried Alfie out of the car and held him up high so that everyone could see it was indeed Alfie.

The welcome home took some time to settle down and it was late in the evening before everyone except Fred had gone home.

But Alfie was worried. There had been no sign of Hack. Was the man mean enough to stay away on purpose?

But Fred said, 'Hack's had a couple of days' leave. But don't worry, he'll be back on duty tomorrow morning. Come on, Alfie, it's bed and a good night's sleep for you.' He led the way to the staffroom where Alfie's basket (and a saucer of creamy milk) awaited him. Alfie lapped up the milk, then jumped into the basket and looked up at Fred. 'Miaow!' he sang happily. It's good to be back. He kneaded the cushion, and turned full circle before setting down.

Fred laughed. 'Goodnight, Alfie,' he said. 'Sweet dreams!'

But Alfie didn't have sweet dreams, he had nightmares about having to face Hack, and wondered whether the man would always hold a grudge against the railway cat.

4

The Competition

Next morning Alfie woke up with a start. Had he overslept? He rushed out of the station just in time to welcome Fred, who was soon followed by Brown. 'My word, Alfie,' said Fred as he bent down to stroke the railway cat. 'Such a relief to have you back on duty.

'We've all been worried about you,' said Brown.

Alfie thought he must be the happiest railway cat in the country – until Brown said, 'Wait until Hack sees you, Alfie. He will be clocking on at eleven o'clock.'

'Miaow!' cried Alfie. I'm not looking forward to meeting *him*.

Soon the staff were fully occupied dealing with passengers. Alfie received so much attention from the children that Fred had difficulty in persuading them to board the train. Drivers leaned out of their cabs and shouted, 'Welcome back, Alfie!'

When it was quiet again, Alfie sat down and started to groom himself. He wasn't going to give Hack the chance to say that the railway cat looked scruffy. Time passed too quickly for Alfie's liking and he started up when Brown called, 'Look out! Here comes Hack.'

Alfie raced off in the direction of the carpark, but Fred sped after him and picked him up. 'Oh, no you don't, Alfie,' he said. 'Hack will want to see you.'

Hack frowned when he saw Alfie struggling to get out of Fred's grip. 'What on earth . . .' he began. 'Don't tell me it's that troublesome cat,' he roared. 'You know I can't bear the sight of him!'

Fred handled Alfie over to Hack who held him tight. He shook Alfie – not too vigorously – and cried, 'You little monster! You wolf in sheep's

clothing! You . . .'

Fred interrupted. 'Are you by any chance talking about our clever, industrious, worth-his-weight-in-gold railway cat, Alfie?'

'I *am*,' cried Hack. 'He's a disaster, a nuisance, a . . .'

But to Alfie's surprise and relief, Hack suddenly burst out laughing and Fred and Brown joined in.

But what was the joke, thought Alfie?

'Well, I was going to tell our Alfie how he helped me win the race at the regatta,' said Hack.

'Go on, then, tell him,' urged Fred.

'Well, I was furious when I saw him running along the towpath, keeping pace with the canoes,' said Hack. 'I guessed he was hissing at me. I dropped the paddle but managed to retrieve it before it floated away.' He paused.

'Go on,' said Fred.

'Thinking: I'll show the little pest what I can do, I paddled as if possessed by a demon. And – I finished *first past the post!*'

Alfie was so amazed at the turn of events that he was unable to miaow.

Hack continued. 'And all because of your antics, Alfie – you little horror . . . you . . .'

'That's enough for today, Hack,' put in Fred, laughing.

'But we're friends now, aren't we?' said Hack.

'Miaow!' said Alfie. Um – yes – well, I'm not so sure . . .

And Fred said hopefully, 'Stay friends for a long, long time, for goodness' sake, so that we can all have a little peace.'

But, sad to report, the peace pact didn't last very long.

Fred had entered the station in the area's Best Kept Station competition and Hack was in charge of the two flowerbeds. Alfie had already noticed how neat and well-kept the beds looked, with a variety of flowering plants in a riot of colour.

Alfie soon became aware that he must keep well clear of Hack for the time being. He had only to stroll near the flowerbeds when, sure enough, Hack would appear. The man must have eyes in the back of his head, thought Alfie.

Hack would shout, 'Keep clear, Alfie, or I'll lock you up,' or, 'Clear off, you little trouble-maker.'

Alfie would feel insulted and mutter 'Brrr . . . brrr . . . brrr . . .'

Fred would shake his head at them and sigh, 'There's never much peace when you two get within sight of one another. I give up!'

One night when he was on patrol Alfie noticed Ginger, the cat from up the road, creeping across the platform. Ha! thought Alfie. He's up to no good.

Alfie gave chase immediately but was not in time to prevent Ginger jumping on to a flower-bed and starting to scratch vigorously at the soil. Soon plants and soil were flying through the air. Battle began as Alfie tried to chase Ginger off the flowerbed before he did any more damage.

It was some time before Alfie managed to box

the enemy's ears and send him packing.

Alfie was dismayed when he examined the damage to the plants. Poor Hack, he thought. The station could only win a booby prize for this flowerbed!

But who was blamed for the damage? Why, poor Alfie, of course! Next morning he listened as Hack shouted at Fred, 'Whatever you say, of course it's Alfie – who else? Wouldn't trust that cat for anything.'

But Fred insisted, 'Alfie would never, *never* behave like that. One of the village cats must be responsible. Pull yourself together, Hack. There are three days to go before the competition, so start straight away to repair the damage. I'll cover your station duties for the next two hours.'

Reluctantly, muttering to himself, Hack set to work and in under two hours the flowerbed looked neat and tidy and attractive again.

'Very good effort, Hack,' said Fred. 'I'm sure the station could win a prize.'

'Huh!' said Hack. 'If only that cat will keep his paws to himself.'

Alfie decided he would stay awake and keep watch during the next three nights. For two nights he lay sleepless, occasionally patrolling the station. All was quiet.

But on the third night he was so tired that he fell fast asleep. He was roused by a familiar scratching sound. He dashed across the platform. Sure enough, there was Ginger sending soil and plants flying. Alfie was so furious he went into action straight away. A fierce skirmish took place and eventually, although thoroughly exhausted, he managed to chase Ginger off the station.

Poor Hack, thought Alfie, as he limped across the platform and lay down under a seat. And

poor me, he thought as he licked an injured paw.

For once, Hack was speechless next morning as he surveyed the damage. But when he did find his voice he let out a yell that could be heard in the village. 'He's done it again! Wait until I catch the little brute, I'll—'

'But you can't blame Alfie without proof,' said Fred. 'I'm sure he is as keen as we are to win the competition.'

Alfie emerged from under a seat and moved forward slowly.

'Just look at him,' cried Hack. 'Might have been dragged through a hedge backwards. And he's limping, which means he's injured a paw scratching at the soil.'

'Nonsense!' said Fred as he bent down to examine Alfie's paw. 'Dear, dear, that's a nasty bite mark. I guess you were trying to protect the plants from someone like old Ginger up the road?'

'Rubbish!' cried Hack.

'Don't you rubbish me, Hack,' retorted Fred.

Hack shuffled his feet and looked sullen. 'Well,' he said, 'I'm having nothing more to do with this stupid competition. You can get someone else to put up with our Alfie's disgraceful behaviour.'

'Now, Hack, just listen to me for a change,' said Fred sternly. 'Alfie is not the culprit and you will enter the competition.'

'No, I won't—' began Hack.

But Fred wasn't listening. His sharp eyes had noticed something sticking up out of the soil. A tin can, perhaps – or, perhaps not?

He picked up a trowel and started to dig. There was a clink of metal against metal and in next to no time Fred had prised his find out of the soil.

'It's an empty beer can,' said Hack, turning away.

'Oh, no, it isn't,' said Fred as he started scraping mud off the object. 'Wait until I've cleaned it up a bit.'

With a resigned expression on his face, and hands in pockets, Hack stood and watched. 'All this fuss and bother just because our Alfie doesn't know how to behave,' he said.

'Oh, keep quiet,' said Fred. 'You may be thanking Alfie soon.'

'Huh! Me thanking him? You must be joking,' said Hack.

But Fred wasn't listening. 'My guess is that this is an engraved silver cup. Here, see what you can make of it.'

Hack took the cup and examined it closely. 'Dates and names,' he cried, 'and *my* name is on it!'

'Well, well,' said Fred. 'My guess is that this is the Station Hotel Snooker Challenge Cup—'

'Yes, yes,' cried Hack, 'it was stolen some months ago. The thief probably buried it here one night, intending to retrieve it after a certain time had passed.'

They looked at one another while Alfie waited hopefully. Had he been forgiven? Ginger obviously enjoyed scratching at the soil so in future he wouldn't try and stop him. Who knows, there might be a *gold* cup hidden further down! That would please Hack, surely?

'Good old Alfie!' shouted Hack at last.

'About time you said that,' cried Fred.

The landlord of the Station Hotel was very pleased when Fred handed him the cup. 'How clever of Alfie to have uncovered it,' he said.

'Huh . . .' said Hack.

'Yes,' put in Fred. 'So what about the competition, Hack?'

'Well . . . well, I suppose I might as well try again,' said Hack – quite cheerfully for him.

'Well done, Hack,' said Fred patting him on the shoulder. 'Take your time, I'll cover your duties.'

The station did not win first prize. However, the judges decided to award a gift token to Hack in appreciation of the work he had done to repair the damaged flowerbeds.

And – guess what? – Hack presented Alfie with a large tail-end of fresh salmon for his part in finding the silver cup!

'My word,' whispered Fred to Alfie, 'things are looking up. But watch your step.'

'Miaow!' cried Alfie. Watch *my* step? What about Hack's step!

'It takes two to make a quarrel,' added Fred wisely.

'Miaow!' agreed Alfie. That's a fact.

5

On Television

It was holiday time and Alfie missed seeing the children. He was very pleased when one morning Fred made an announcement to the staff (including Alfie, of course).

'Our station is to be used again for a brief episode in a new television comedy,' said Fred.

'Miaow!' sang Alfie.

'Whoopee!' cried Brown.

'Means more work for us, I suppose,' said Hack.

Fred ignored him.

Alfie remembered the previous filming – how friendly the director, cameramen and cast had been, and the excitement of watching the actual filming.

'It's up to us to see that everything goes like clockwork, so I'll give you a few details. Everybody listening?' said Fred.

'What a stupid que–' began Hack.

'What did you say?' interrupted Fred sharply.

'Sorry,' mumbled Hack hastily.

Fred continued:

'One. They will arrive at approximately eight o'clock next Monday morning.

'Two. Platform Number 2 will be closed to the public all morning.

'Three. Local trains will be diverted and the nine o'clock express from London – by special permission from headquarters – will stop at Number 2 platform for the filming.'

He paused. 'Any questions?'

Hack spoke up, 'What are we supposed to be doing?'

'Do as you are told,' was Fred's prompt reply.

Alfie was up bright and early next Monday morning. After breakfast he sat in the carpark to await his friends. In due course Brown called from the booking-office, 'Any minute now, Alfie.'

Soon, two large vehicles drew up and the director, first to step out, greeted Alfie. 'Believe me, Alfie, I would have gone straight back home if you had not been here to welcome us.'

'Prrr . . . prrr . . . prrr . . .' said Alfie, rubbing his head against the man's leg.

Back in the station Fred whispered to Alfie, 'You can stay here and watch, but keep out of the way at all costs.'

'Miaow!' cried Alfie indignantly. I know how to behave. He was determined not to miss one second of the filming.

The director made an announcement. 'This is going to be a very short but important part of the film. The young man will be waiting on the platform for his girlfriend to arrive on the London train. When the train comes in, he sees the girl waving from an open carriage window. Train stops, he rushes forward to open carriage door and – er – well, you'll have to see for yourselves what happens next.'

'Sounds stupid to me,' muttered Hack under his breath.

At that moment Alfie thought he saw a mouse and dashed across the platform in pursuit.

'Look at that cat!' shouted Leading Railman Hack. 'Making a nuisance of himself as usual. I'll catch him and lock him up. I'll—'

'Oh, no, you won't,' snapped the director as he barred Hack's path. 'What's wrong with an intelligent, well-mannered railway cat being here? Most natural thing in the world. Station wouldn't function without your Alfie.'

Unable to locate the mouse, Alfie had returned in time to hear the last sentence.

'Miaow!' he agreed. We railway cats do have our responsibilities.

The director gave orders – actors to be dressed and made up, cameras to be in position, lighting to be attended to, etcetera. Alfie loved all the hustle and bustle.

By ten o'clock everyone concerned had assembled on platform Number 2. The actors – two in railway uniform, the young man and a few passengers – waited for the incoming train.

Soon Fred called out, 'Train approaching.'

'Ready for action everyone,' said the director.

As the train came in a young woman standing at an open window waved to the young man. He rushed forward and opened the carriage door. She handed him a suitcase which he put down before helping her out of the train.

They embraced. He kissed her, then she kissed him – then he kissed her again.

'This is getting monotonous,' said Hack, pretending to yawn.

'Shush!' warned Fred.

The young woman looked round nervously then, without warning, she picked up the suitcase and made a dash back to the train. He grabbed her and they argued as he tried to lead her towards the exit. Eventually she managed to push him aside, heave the case into the train and jump in after it. She slammed the door.

The train moved off as the young man rushed up to the window and, waving his fist shouted, 'Good riddance.'

The director looked worried and shook his head.

'Boring, absolutely bor–' began Hack loudly.

Fred turned on him. 'If I have to tell you again, you'll be suspended,' he said.

The cameras kept on rolling as the young man started to run off, but he halted as a raucous wolf-like whistle was heard. Alfie pricked up his ears.

Was it? Could it possibly be? Yes, yes, he was sure it was his friend Nikki, the bright green and red parrot from the Station Hotel, who had been missing for three months.

But there was no sign of the bird. Where could he be hiding? Then came, 'SQUAWK! SQUAWK! SQUAWK!' and Nikki emerged from under a seat. He fluffed out his chest and fluttered towards Alfie, who rushed to meet his friend.

Hack gave chase. Alfie turned suddenly. Hack tripped over him and they both lay sprawled on the platform as the cameras kept on rolling.

All was confusion and, to make matters worse, as Hack tried to get on his feet, Nikki landed on his head! The parrot then started pulling Hack's hair with his claws.

'OUCH! OUCH! OUCH!' yelled Hack. 'CLEAR OFF!'

Nikki opened his beak wide and Alfie guessed what was coming for the parrot knew only one sentence, which he used to repeat over and over again at the hotel.

Sure enough Nikki started calling, 'GET LOST YOU SILLY OLD CODGER! GET LOST YOU SILLY OLD CODGER! GET

LOST YOU SILLY OLD CODGER!'

Fred put his hands to his head. 'I expect I'll be blamed for all this chaos,' he moaned.

Hack was still dancing about trying to get Nikki off his head. Fred managed to grab the parrot and held him tight.

'The film has been ruined,' cried Fred. 'I don't know what the director will say. By the way, where is he?' He turned round and saw the director sitting on a seat. His hands covered his face and his shoulders shook.

'Miaow!' said Alfie. What a disaster for the poor man.

Fred went up to the director. 'Believe me, sir,' he began. 'We're all very sorry. The parrot doesn't belong to us, so we're not to blame for that.'

The director continued to shake.

Fred tried again. 'We're really really sorry,' he said anxiously, putting a hand on the man's shoulder. We're all sorry.'

The director took his hands from his face and the tears rolled down his cheeks. 'Sorry?' he gulped. 'Stop saying, "Sorry", for goodness' sake. Sorry!'

He fumbled for a handkerchief as the tears continued to flow. Then, worse still, he started to laugh. Hysterical, prolonged laughter – and he couldn't stop.

'Miaow!' said Alfie, looking up at Fred. He's gone off his head!

Fred had obviously come to the same conclusion. Saying, 'We'd better get a doctor quickly,' he started off towards the office.

But the director put out a hand and stuttered, 'St–o–p, stop. Don't you understand? This episode will make the film a great success. It's the fun – fun – funniest thing I've ever – ever – ' He couldn't continue for laughing again.

And everyone joined in.

'We'll probably win an award for this film,' said the director. 'And all thanks due to Alfie and the parrot. Alfie should have been an actor.'

Alfie was very pleased, but he said, 'Miaow!' Thank you for the compliment, but I'd rather be the railway cat.

And Hack said, 'Huh! That cat could never be a successful actor. He's a menace. Ought to be pensioned off.'

'Miaow!' hissed Alfie. I'm not an old cat and it wasn't my fault you fell over.

After the director and his team had departed everyone could talk of nothing else but the film.

'But I still don't understand what it was all about,' insisted Hack.

'You'll have the answer to that when you see the film on television,' said Fred. 'And, take my word for it, I know who will be a favourite character.'

'Well, I'm glad you recognise my talent,' said Hack smugly.

'Not you – Alfie!' cried Fred. 'He'll be a star all right.'

'You're joking,' said Hack. 'That cat's more like a striped bundle of rubbish than a star.'

'Miaow!' snarled Alfie.

But then he acknowledged to himself that Hack had been very funny (quite unintentionally, of course) so Alfie stretched up and licked Hack's hand to show his appreciation.

But Hack pushed him away.

'Oh, don't be so mean, Hack,' cried Fred.

Somewhat reluctantly Hack bent down and stroked Alfie – and actually tickled him under the chin! Alfie really enjoyed this rare attention from Hack.

'Friends now, I hope,' said Fred, beaming.

'So long as he keeps well out of my way,' said Hack.

'I give up,' sighed Fred, who was still holding Nikki.

A man came running on to the platform.

'Oh, hello, Mr Smith,' cried Fred. 'You've heard about your Nikki's safe return, have you?' He handed the parrot over to his owner.

'Thank you, Fred,' said Mr Smith, as he gently stroked the bird's head. 'I can't tell you how relieved I am to have Nikki back. I'll take him home straight away. Coming with us, Alfie?'

'Miaow!' sang Alfie. Certainly. I know where I am always welcome.

And as he followed Mr Smith and Nikki into the hotel the parrot started screaming, 'GET LOST YOU SILLY OLD CODGER! GET LOST . . .'

'Miaow!' grumbled Alfie. I really do wish Mr Smith would teach you to say something else for a change.

When Mr Smith had attended to Nikki, Alfie followed him into the kitchen, where he was sure there would be a tasty morsel waiting for him.

And he was not disappointed.

Another Hodder Children's book

THE RAILWAY CAT'S SECRET

Phyllis Arkle

Fred has a secret. And whatever it is, it's making Alfie the railway cat's life a misery. Fred has no time for a chat any more.

Then Alfie discovered a little station further down the track – with its own special secret! Alfie's determined not to let anyone find it – but then some unexpected visitors arrive and nobody has a secret any more!